INVISIBLE SIX 6

FLIGHT OF THE VULTURE

JIM CORRIGAN

An Imprint of
Srishti Publishers & Distributors

For Sgt. Maj. James G. Sartor of the 10th Special Forces Group (Airborne), who died from enemy small arms fire in Faryab Province, Afghanistan, on July 13, 2019. —JC

For my invisible backup team, Louis, Rory, Evie, and Heather. Without them, no mission gets off the ground. —KH

Srishti Publishers & Distributors
A unit of AJR Publishing LLP
212A, Peacock Lane
Shahpur Jat, New Delhi – 110 049
editorial@srishtipublishers.com

First published in India by
Srishti Publishers & Distributors in 2023

First Published by Abdo Publishing,
a division of ABDO Publishing Company in 2022

Copyright © Abdo Consulting Group Inc, 2022
10 9 8 7 6 5 4 3 2 1

This is a work of fiction. The characters, places, organisations and events described in this book are either a work of the author's imagination or have been used fictitiously. Any resemblance to people, living or dead, places, events, communities or organisations is purely coincidental.
The author asserts the moral right to be identified as the author of this work.

All rights reserved. No part of this publication may be reproduced, stored in a retrieval system, or transmitted, in any form or by any means, electronic, mechanical, photocopying, recording or otherwise, without the prior written permission of the Publishers.

Claw™ is a trademark and logo of Abdo Publishing Company,
PO Box 398166, Minneapolis, Minnesota 55439, USA.
All rights reserved.

This edition is for sale in India only
Printed and bound in India

TABLE OF CONTENTS

INVISIBLE SIX PERSONNEL

Athena

Role: Team Leader
Service History: Operations staff, 75th Ranger Regiment. Squadron commander, Delta Force.
Profile: Excels at tactics and strategy. Handles herself well in a firefight, but her time is best spent planning and maintaining situational awareness.

Shade

Role: Executive Officer
Service History: CIA Special Operations Group.
Profile: Recruited by the CIA right out of high school. Extensively trained in spy craft and covert ops. Businesslike and loyal.

Doc Dee

Role: Medic
Service History: Medical Department, USS *America* amphibious assault ship.
Profile: Believes in the unit's purpose but gives priority to his doctor's oath. Interested in all the arts and sciences, enabling him to offer out-of-the-box solutions.

Gizmo

Role: Tech Specialist
Service History: National Security Agency.
Profile: Recruited by software companies and the NSA after getting caught writing illegal modifications for video games. Solves problems in eavesdropping, countersurveillance, and codebreaking.

Zumi

Role: Jumpmaster/Rescuer/Mechanic
Service History: Puerto Rico Air National Guard, US Air Force Special Operations Command.
Profile: Joined the Air Guard to work on heavy equipment and parachute jump. Graduate and instructor of the Air Force pararescue school.

Bicep

Role: Infantryman
Service History: US Naval Special Warfare Command.
Profile: Accepted into Navy SEAL training, but dropped out for family reasons. Later returned to the Navy and joined Special Warfare Group 4. Serves as the team's parachute rigger and maritime expert.

TOP SECRET
(YOUR EYES ONLY)

From:

General Ledlie, Pentagon

To:

Special Operative ZUMI

Mission Codename:

NOBLE SNARE

I am approving a CIA request to deploy Invisible Six on a special mission. Your target is the notorious terrorist Viggo the Vulture. As you know, Viggo has left a worldwide trail of innocent victims. After his most recent attack, launched from US soil, the CIA tracked him to a desert outpost. Viggo is hiding there right now. The cold-blooded killer must be stopped at all costs.

- Raid VIGGO THE VULTURE'S secret base of operations.
- Apprehend him alive, if at all possible.
- Seize all terrorist intel discovered at the base.

CHAPTER 1

FATEFUL DECISIONS

1,400 Meters above
Boston Harbor
0715 Local / 12 JUL

Zumi knelt on the deck of the HH-60 Pave Hawk helicopter, surrounded by her students. The four men and women were training to become pararescue jumpers, or PJs. In their eyes, Zumi saw focus and determination. This group was nearly ready. Today's training—a water-rescue operation—would challenge them.

"After you jump, swim directly to your assigned victims," Zumi said into her helmet's microphone. "Assess their injuries and keep them safe until it's your turn to use the winch and basket."

The students listened intently on their headsets.

"Once all victims have been hoisted aboard, climb the rope ladder—"

"Ma'am," the aircraft commander broke in on the intercom, "we have a situation you need to know about. A 737 passenger jet out of Logan International has just declared an emergency. It may need to make a water landing."

Zumi glanced out the helicopter's open door to a clear blue sky and sapphire harbor. She made a snap decision. "Understood. Advise air traffic control you have five PJs on board who can assist with rescue operations."

"Roger that."

Zumi looked to her students and said,

"Graduation is coming a little early. I know your abilities. You can do this."

The helicopter turned and accelerated. Air traffic control was routing them to the potential crash site.

A streak of black, oily smoke marred the perfect sky. Zumi's eyes followed it to the stricken airliner. As they drew closer, she spotted scorch marks on the jet's belly and tail. The helicopter pulled alongside. Zumi knew the 737 pilots were reducing speed to bare minimum. Now, at just one hundred fifty meters above the water, they kept the jet's nose slightly elevated.

"That's it," Zumi whispered. "Set it down nice and easy."

The next few seconds were critical. Zumi watched the jet's belly ease onto the water. The wings and fuselage shuddered.

White sea-foam flew in sheets. The jet's nose touched down, forcing an abrupt stop. Its tail lurched up and then slapped the water. The jet had landed in one piece.

Zumi saw the emergency doors pop open. Passengers began streaming onto the wings and into the water.

"Take us in," Zumi told the helicopter pilots. Then she turned to her students. "A plane with a hole in its belly will sink like a brick. Get everyone out and then tend to the injured."

They nodded. Zumi assigned two students to each wing exit. She would take the forward door herself.

"These people are terrified," she added. "Calm them with your professionalism."

The helicopter hovered just a few meters from the water's surface, dropping PJs at their positions.

Zumi watched her students jump. Then it was her turn. She stood at the deck's edge with her arms crossed. Then she plunged into the water and began kicking furiously for the aircraft. She passed clusters of people in yellow life vests.

"Rescue boats are on the way," she yelled to them.

A flight attendant came down the forward exit's evacuation slide.

"How many more on board?" Zumi asked.

"Just the captain," the attendant said. "He's making a final check."

Zumi scrambled up the slide. "Captain?" she called.

The cockpit was empty. So was first-class seating. Zumi started down the aisle toward a wall of water, which had already claimed the aft section.

"Captain!" she shouted.

A man in a white shirt with pilot's epaulets emerged from the water. He pushed aside bobbing luggage and seat cushions.

"I had to be sure we got them all," he said, coughing.

Zumi extended an arm. "Come with me. It's time to go."

They hurried up the aisle. In first class, the water was thigh-deep. The evacuation slide had come loose and drifted away. They stepped straight into the bay and swam a safe distance, then turned to watch the plane's nose vanish underwater.

"Do you have any idea what happened?" Zumi asked.

"It was a SAM," the captain said grimly.

Zumi arched an eyebrow. Surface-to-air missiles were weapons of war, designed

to protect ground forces from air attacks. "Why do you suspect a missile?"

"It's not my first time being shot at," he explained. "I flew F-16s over Iraq. Got a tail full of shrapnel once. This impact felt the same. Trust me, it was a SAM."

Coast Guard cutters arrived, along with some fishing boats. The vessels began plucking people from the water. Zumi's students cared for the injured with skill, filling her with pride. A head count confirmed everyone had been recovered.

Later, Zumi stood with the airline captain on the deck of a rescue boat, watching air bubbles emerge from the sunken jet. Feelings of pride and relief evaporated as she considered the cause. It was, after all, no accident. Someone had gone to great effort to shoot down the jet. The thought enraged her.

"A planeload of civilians." The captain shook his head. "Who would do such a thing?"

Zumi frowned. "I plan to find out."

CIA Headquarters
Langley, Virginia
0930 Local / 15 JUL

An aide met Shade and Zumi in the lobby, then ushered them upstairs to a conference room.

"The director of counterterrorism will be with you shortly," the aide said before closing the door.

Zumi had not known what to expect during her first visit to the CIA. Aside from tight security, it seemed like any office space, full of cubicles and meeting rooms.

"How long did you work here?" she asked Shade.

"I never spent much time at Langley," he replied. "The agency recruited me right out of high school. They oversaw my higher education and military training, then assigned me to a black ops team."

"Do you know the person we're meeting?"

Shade nodded. "Director Ngata is shrewd and perceptive. Be ready to back up your opinions with facts."

The door opened. A tall woman in a blue business suit entered.

"Good to see you, Shade," she said, smiling. "How are things at I-6? Are you ready to come home yet?"

Shade grinned. “I’d like to introduce you to one of my I-6 colleagues, call sign Zumi.”

“An honor,” Ngata said. “I’m aware of your work at Boston Harbor. Nicely done.”

“Thank you, ma’am,” Zumi said.

“So,” the director said as they took their seats, “I have information you may find interesting.”

She produced a pocket projector and set it on the table. The projector beamed a satellite image of Boston Harbor onto the wall. “We’ve confirmed that a shoulder-launched SAM was fired from a bayside rooftop. The missile was an SA-18 Grouse.”

“Do you have suspects?” Shade asked.

Ngata tapped a button for the next slide. The grainy image showed a bearded man in sunglasses carrying a long case.

"A security cam caught this man in the suspected launch area," she explained. "Our analysts say it is Viggo the Vulture."

Shade clasped his hands. "Viggo has been on everyone's most wanted list for years. Nobody knows his real name. I didn't even know we had photos of him."

"This is the first," Ngata said. "And it's a huge breakthrough. Using advanced algorithms and facial-recognition tech, we've tracked the Vulture to his nest."

She displayed another satellite image, this time of a desert outpost. A high wall surrounded the building. A single vehicle sat parked behind the gate.

"Viggo went here after leaving Boston," she said. "It's deep in the Sahara Desert, one of the harshest regions in the world."

Zumi leaned forward. "Let's get him."

"No need," Ngata said, waving a hand.

"He's alone in that compound. We can destroy it with a drone strike."

"Any idea why he shot down an airliner?" Shade asked.

"Most terrorists are motivated by ideology, but not Viggo," Ngata said. "His only concern is money. He recently acquired a stockpile of SA-18 missiles. Now he needs to sell them. The jet was a demonstration for potential buyers."

"Are you serious?" Shade fumed. "He shot down a plane full of people as a sales gimmick?"

Ngata nodded. "He enjoys showing off for his terrorist clients."

Zumi's mind flashed back to all those frightened faces in the water. They had been the lucky ones. Viggo's victims rarely lived to tell of the experience.

"We need to go get him," Zumi said.

"No, we need to kill him," said the director. "I have an MQ-9 Reaper on its way to his hideout. In a few hours, four Hellfire air-to-ground missiles will blast that compound into rubble."

"That's the safe play," Zumi said. "You'd eliminate a deadly terrorist. But how soon until another one takes his place? What if we used this opportunity to do more?"

Ngata's eyes narrowed. "What are you proposing?"

Zumi rose and walked to the projected image of the desert outpost. "Every businessperson, even an illegal-arms dealer, needs to keep records. I'll bet this building contains precious information. The identity of his missile supplier, for example, and the locations of his clients."

"It'd be a shame to lose that valuable intel in a drone strike," Shade noted.

Zumi continued, “I-6 could make a night raid. We’d take the Vulture into custody, then grab every bit of data we can find.”

Ngata sat back in her chair. “And then?”

“Then you can close down a huge part of the underground weapons market.”

“I’m asking about Viggo,” the director said. “What would you do once he’s in custody?”

Zumi considered the question. “I’d make him answer for his crimes. Put him on trial at the International Criminal Court, where his victims’ families could confront him.”

Silence followed as Ngata considered the proposal. Zumi knew it was a big risk. If the raid went sideways, Viggo might escape to kill again.

“What you’re asking me for is trust,”

Ngata said. "Frankly, trust doesn't come easy in my profession."

Shade leaned forward. "Ma'am, you know my service history. I've had the honor of working with some truly elite teams. I can tell you that I-6 is the finest."

The director regarded Shade for a long moment. Then she snatched the projector. "Prepare for rapid deployment. I'll square it with General Ledlie."

They watched Ngata go. Then Shade let out a deep breath. "I hope you realize the risk of this mission. You've signed us up for a big gamble."

"No choice," Zumi said gravely. "Viggo needs to answer for his crimes."

CHAPTER 2

LONG RIDE DOWN

10,000 Meters above
the Sahara Desert
2315 Local / 16 JUL

After receiving their orders, Zumi and Shade had picked up the rest of the team. Now, I-6 huddled in a C-17 Globemaster cargo plane flying high above Sudan. They were engrossed in mission prep.

Zumi, as the team's jumpmaster, handled details of their insertion by parachute. To keep Viggo from hearing the jet's engines and escaping, they would make a high-altitude jump. They had two choices. A low-opening jump, or HALO, would provide a rapid descent via free fall. A high-opening jump, or HAHO, meant a lengthy drift beneath the parachute. The difference boiled down to speed versus precision.

"This mission calls for HAHO," Zumi told the team. "The long ride down will let us steer directly into Viggo's compound."

"If you land outside the wall, don't sweat it," Athena added. "The first person to land inside it will open the gate."

Shade, who was applying camouflage face paint, looked up from his mirror. "Noise discipline is essential. With luck, we'll catch the Vulture asleep in his bed."

"He has no guards?" Bicep asked.

"Our intel says he's alone," Athena said. "CIA analysts believe Viggo is super paranoid, trusting only himself. Still, we should be ready for anything."

"What are the rules of engagement?" Gizmo asked.

"We'll try to take him alive, but if he refuses, that's his choice," Athena said. "Once the site is secure, we'll gather up all intel and call for extraction. Two choppers will be waiting in the desert."

I-6 readied to jump. Earth's cold, thin upper atmosphere could be deadly. The team pulled on warm, windproof clothing and face masks with oxygen hoses. Zumi handed out oxygen bottles and checked the hose connections. Nobody could jump until she'd inspected his or her safety gear and given a thumbs-up.

The overhead lights dimmed. Zumi flicked on her visor's night vision, which bathed the cargo bay in ghostly green. She also activated her wrist-mounted altimeter and GPS unit. These devices linked to the helmet and projected their data directly onto her visor.

The plane's ramp lowered. The team gazed out into the moonless night. Stars glowed brightly on Zumi's visor, but the desert below was a featureless void. She waited for the target to appear.

A green dot pulsed, marking the coordinates of Viggo's base. Zumi walked down the ramp and stepped into free fall.

She stabilized into a facedown position, then looked over her shoulder. The rest of the team was in the air, and the C-17 was flying off. Her visor showed an altitude of nine thousand meters. Zumi let it get to eight thousand before pulling the rip cord. Again, she checked the status of her teammates. After seeing five more chutes open, she turned her attention to steering.

As she drifted toward the green dot on her visor, Zumi cleared her mind. The first few minutes on the ground would require laser-like focus. Viggo's hideout became her entire world. Until it was secured, nothing else mattered.

Soon the green dot pulsed beneath her feet. She switched off her GPS as the compound came into view.

Zumi realized that she had placed herself directly over the building. A rooftop landing could alert Viggo. With a few gentle tugs, she moved off to one side. She flared the canopy just before touching down, making a soft, silent landing inside the compound.

Zumi detached the chute and drew her weapon. She was on her way to unlock the gate when Bicep passed overhead. He landed less gracefully, tumbling into the muck of an animal pen. Zumi stifled a laugh as a goat sniffed Bicep's face.

I-6 assembled near Viggo's SUV. Then they split into two teams. Athena, Zumi, and Gizmo would breach the building's northern door, while the other team would enter from the south. CIA analysts had advised against trying to pick the locks. Viggo's paranoia would mean vibration sensors and tamper-resistant doors.

Athena slid a GREM grenade onto the muzzle of her M4 carbine. The GREM's odd shape reminded Zumi of a lawn dart, but its effectiveness was beyond question. The breach grenade could flatten a door from thirty meters away.

"Ready north," Athena said over the communications network.

"Ready south," Shade replied from the other side of the building.

"Execute."

The breach grenade slammed into the door and exploded, leaving a gaping hole. Gizmo and Zumi rushed through, their infrared lasers probing a smoky hallway. The other team appeared through the splintered doorway on the hall's far side. Zumi pointed her weapon up an elegant wooden staircase but saw no movement.

"South team, clear this level," Athena ordered. "We'll go upstairs."

Shade's team fanned across the first floor, while Athena started up the stairway with Zumi and Gizmo close behind.

Viggo clearly enjoyed a life of luxury. Zumi's boots trod on fine Persian carpet. A staircase landing featured a gold vulture on a marble pedestal. The rooms had plush furniture and opulent wall art.

"Jackpot," Athena said when they

discovered Viggo's business office. She examined a laptop sitting on a mahogany desk. "We'll strip this room clean."

The staccato of automatic-weapons fire came from downstairs. They heard shouting. A door slammed. They ran from the office and vaulted down the stairs.

Bicep paced the hallway with his rifle trained on a closed door. "Viggo went in there. Shade's been hit."

They found Shade sprawled across a dining room table with Doc Dee bent over him. Bullet holes pocked the walls.

"Report," Athena said.

"Viggo came out of nowhere," Doc Dee said. "He opened up on us. I think he wanted to make a break for it, but he couldn't get past us, so he ran into the basement."

Shade was unconscious. Doc Dee used

scissors to cut open his blood-soaked shirt.

"Is he going to be okay?" Zumi asked. Dread gnawed at her belly.

"I don't know," Doc Dee said, his hands moving quickly. "We need to get him out of here."

Athena plucked the radio from her hip. "Desert Eagle, this is Nomad requesting emergency evac. Be advised that we have one wounded in action. Condition critical."

"Copy, Nomad," replied the helicopter commander. "This is Desert Eagle, on our way. Ten-minute ETA."

Athena turned to Gizmo. "You and Bicep need to pack up what you can from that office. Give top priority to electronics. You only have ten minutes, so hurry."

"What about Viggo?" Gizmo asked.

"Zumi and I will handle him. Now go!"

Gizmo and Bicep bolted. Athena turned to Zumi. "Let's go get this guy."

Zumi tamped down her concern for Shade and focused on the mission. She followed Athena into the hallway.

The wooden cellar door yielded to a good kick. They descended into a storeroom of illegal arms. Rows of crates climbed to the ceiling. Zumi saw land mines and flamethrowers, but no Viggo.

"Where'd he go?" whispered Athena.

Zumi went to a corner. "Look at this."

A crate of rockets had been pushed aside, revealing a small, square exit. Zumi dropped to her hands and knees. "It's an escape tunnel."

Outside, a car engine roared to life. They sprinted up the stairs and through the shattered doorway, just in time to see Viggo's SUV speed away.

CHAPTER 3

EMERGENCY SURGERY

USS *Harry S. Truman*
Mediterranean Sea
0730 Local / 17 JUL

Navy corpsmen carried Shade's stretcher from the helicopter. Doc Dee ran alongside, holding up a bag of blood plasma. Zumi watched with concern.

"I'll let you know as soon as I can," Doc Dee yelled over his shoulder before disappearing belowdecks.

As the rest of the team crossed the busy, windswept flight deck, the ship's captain came down from the bridge. "Our medical facilities are the finest in the

fleet," she assured them. "We're equipped for almost any surgery."

"Thanks, skipper," said Athena. "Have your aircraft had any luck tracking Viggo?"

The captain shook her head. "We're still scouring the desert."

The four worried teammates stowed their gear and gathered outside Shade's operating room. The *Truman*'s thousands of sailors and aviators kept the little hospital busy. In an adjacent OR, a young seaman was undergoing an appendectomy. I-6 waited in a gray corridor as medical staff streamed past.

Zumi's mind flashed back to the CIA meeting at Langley. She had talked Director Ngata out of the drone strike. If she'd kept her mouth shut, Shade would be fine and Viggo would be dead.

The OR doors swung open. Corpsmen

wheeled Shade to the recovery room. Doc Dee and the ship's surgeon emerged. They conferred briefly and shook hands. Zumi held her breath as Doc Dee approached the group.

"The bullet missed his vital organs," he told them. "We've stopped the internal bleeding. Shade will need time to heal, but he's going to be okay."

Everyone exhaled and exchanged haggard smiles. Zumi felt a weight lift from her shoulders. Problems remained, but the nightmare scenario had been avoided.

"Let's clear out, people," said Athena. "Shade needs his rest, and so do we. Grab some food and get a few hours of sleep."

"Then what?" Zumi asked.

Athena's eyes were determined. "Then we figure out our next move."

6

Naval Air Station Sigonella
Sicily, Italy
1615 Local / 19 JUL

A V-22 Osprey had flown the team from the *Truman* to the naval air station. Shade had slept for most of the way on a stretcher. Now, as they waited in an aircraft hangar, Shade was awake, alert, and full of questions about the plan.

"Run through it from the beginning," he said, propping himself up on his elbows.

Doc Dee gently pushed his shoulders back down. "Your mission is to recover. I've arranged a private suite for you at Walter Reed Medical Center."

"Look, I'm still I-6's exec officer," Shade said. "I'll rest easier knowing the plan."

Athena looked to Doc Dee, who reluctantly nodded.

"We're renewing our pursuit of the Vulture," Athena said. "We're going wherever his trail takes us."

Shade looked skeptical. "After his close call with us, Viggo will stay in hiding. I know I would."

"We thought that too," Athena said. "But Viggo is a businessman with dangerous clients. Any terrorists who fail to receive their weapons will come looking for him."

"And unlike us, they'll want to do more than just capture him," Bicep added.

"So, he needs to get back to business," Shade mused. "But how will you pick up his trail?"

"With this." Gizmo held up a flash drive. "It's the contents of Viggo's laptop. I made a copy before we shipped the captured intel to Langley."

Shade's eyes widened. "It's decoded?"

Gizmo grinned. "Bruh, this data is like an X-ray into the illegal-arms trade. We've got names and locations from around the world."

"Okay, I'm impressed," Shade said. "But how do you infiltrate the most dangerous black market on the planet? Arms dealers won't welcome a US special ops team."

The others started laughing.

"What's so funny?" Shade asked.

Athena unzipped a satchel. "Director Ngata sent this."

Shade rummaged through the bag. "Cash, fake passports, cryptocurrency keys. Wait, you're going undercover?"

“We’ll pose as mercenaries,” Bicep said. “Our imaginary employer is looking to buy SA-18 missiles.”

Shade gave a half smile. “It makes sense. Black-market buyers and sellers often use a go-between for safety.”

“We just need to wave that money around and watch the arms dealers come running,” Gizmo said.

“There’s only one problem,” Shade said. “Your CIA-trained teammate, an expert in spy craft, is confined to a stretcher.”

“And that’s where he’s staying,” Doc Dee said. “The surgeon and I spent too much time putting you back together.”

“We’ll keep you in the loop,” Athena promised. “Look, here comes your ride.”

A C-37A jet of the 76th Airlift Squadron pulled into the hangar. The team said their goodbyes. Doc Dee went ahead to speak with the flight crew, while Zumi wheeled Shade over to the little jet.

“You’ve been quiet,” Shade said as she pushed the stretcher.

Zumi hesitated. She didn’t know what to say. But then the words came out. “I screwed up, and I’m sorry.”

“I don’t think you screwed up,” Shade said. “And you have nothing to be sorry about.”

“You got shot because of me.”

“No.” He looked back at her. “I got shot because a terrorist fired a gun at me. It’s a hazard of our work.”

Zumi shook her head.

“Listen,” Shade said. “This is a key mission. The intel we captured will save innocent lives. So will catching Viggo.”

“You warned me of the risks,” Zumi said.

"We don't do risk-free missions. Look, I'm fine," Shade insisted. "Or at least I will be once I get a new ball cap."

Zumi smiled. Shade had lost his trademark baseball cap during the raid. Before leaving the *Truman*, Zumi had visited the ship's store and bought him a replacement. Now, she reached into her rucksack and handed it to him.

"Oh, thanks," he said, running his fingers across the stitched aircraft carrier on the front of the cap.

They reached the jet, where a pair of airmen waited to take Shade aboard.

"Listen, you'll need to assist Athena while I'm gone," he said while putting on the cap. "But don't get any ideas about taking the exec job. I'll be back before you know it."

CHAPTER 4

SCORPION STING

Unknown Location
Ethiopia
1445 Local / 20 JUL

The I-6 team, minus Shade, sat unarmed and blindfolded in the back of a rumbling old cargo truck. It was the only way to meet the well-connected arms dealer known as Scorpion. Their weapons would be returned after the meeting, supposedly.

The team had dressed as mercenaries. Instead of matching uniforms, they now wore an eclectic mix of military and civilian clothing. Zumi's new combat boots came from France. A German knife was strapped to her calf, hidden beneath American blue jeans.

Scorpion's guards had missed the knife. Now, it was the team's only weapon.

The truck jerked to a stop. Zumi heard the rhythmic gunfire of a rifle range. Somebody yanked off the blindfold. She reached for her sunglasses, then jumped from the truck. Scorpion's guards hurried her and the team past rows of canvas tents and into a decrepit factory.

Zumi whistled. The sprawling factory held more weapons than most armories. She picked up an Uzi submachine gun.

"I have a special deal on those," called a man with a thick accent. "Highest quality. You wish to buy five? I can give you an excellent deal."

"Thanks," said Athena, "but we're shopping on behalf of a client."

"Of course, a discreet purchase," said Scorpion. "What item is needed?"

"Surface-to-air missiles."

"Very expensive," said the weapons dealer. "You have money?"

Athena opened her satchel, revealing the cash. He nodded and then led them to a second building. Scorpion was a natural salesman, chatty and gregarious. His thick arms flailed as he touted his latest deals on mortar tubes and body armor.

"Just the missiles," said Athena.

Inside the second building, he led them down a long aisle of missiles and launchers. Athena scanned the inventory.

"Our client is looking for the SA-18 Grouse," she said. "Do you have any?"

Scorpion picked up a launcher. "I have an SA-16 Gimlet. Just as good."

Athena wrinkled her nose. "Thanks,

but our client really wants the 18. Do you know where we can get it?"

He held up a hand. "The 18 is overrated. Look at this Stinger missile. Highest quality."

"Very nice," Athena said, "but we need the 18. I'd be happy to pay you a finder's fee for introducing us to a seller."

Scorpion's smile disappeared. "Finder's fee," he grumbled.

"One thousand US dollars," Athena said brightly. "Just tell us where to find an SA-18 dealer."

"Excuse me, please," he said, stepping away to murmur into his cell phone.

Zumi heard a door swing open, followed by footsteps. Armed men surrounded the team. Scorpion's smile returned, but this time it was sinister. He yanked the satchel from Athena.

"So picky," he sneered. "Now your client gets nothing, and you must work for me."

At his command, guards took them to a windowless room and shoved them to the floor, then cinched zip ties around their wrists and ankles. The guards slammed the door. Their footsteps faded.

"Scorpion needs to work on his customer service skills," said Bicep.

"I have a knife hidden under my left pant leg," Zumi said.

Athena and Doc Dee shimmied across the filthy floor. Together, they managed to roll up the pant leg and unsheathe the knife. Doc Dee gripped the knife handle as Athena carefully moved her wrist tie across the razor-sharp blade. Her hands came loose. Moments later, everyone was free. Athena handed the knife to Bicep, who quietly worked on the door lock.

"Here's the plan," Athena said. "Gizmo and Bicep will go find some firepower. The rest of us will pay a visit to Scorpion."

Bicep opened the door and poked his head into the hallway, then signaled the all clear. He handed Zumi her knife.

"Execute," Athena whispered.

They crept into the hallway. Gizmo and Bicep headed toward the aisles of weapons, while everyone else followed the warble of Scorpion's voice. They found him in his office, speaking into his phone about the virtues of anti-tank mines.

Zumi brandished the tactical knife. Scorpion dropped his phone.

"Where can we find Viggo the Vulture?" Athena asked, grabbing her satchel from the desk.

Scorpion's eyes narrowed. "Americans. You seek revenge for the airliner."

"Where is Viggo?" Athena demanded.

"You will never find him," Scorpion said.

Zumi edged closer. "This blade is stainless steel," she said through gritted teeth. "Highest quality."

"Okay, okay," Scorpion said. He slowly opened a desk drawer and looked to Zumi for permission to reach inside. When she nodded, Scorpion took out a business card with nothing but GPS coordinates. "Your best chance is here, at the Showroom."

"What's the Showroom?" asked Zumi.

"A secret place where dealers can display weapons for sale. Very classy."

Gunfire erupted in the hallway.

Gizmo rushed into the office with an armful of Israeli Tavor-21 assault rifles. "The guards spotted us. Bicep is holding them off for now."

Scorpion chortled. "My men will shoot you like rabid dogs."

"Bruh, we can handle ourselves."

"Let's take Scorpion with us," Zumi suggested. She re-sheathed her knife and slapped a magazine into a Tavor. "They won't risk shooting their boss."

The arms dealer's smile disappeared.

Athena turned to Gizmo. "We're coming out, and we're bringing Scorpion with us. Be ready to move."

"Roger." Gizmo rushed from the office.

Zumi, Athena, and Doc Dee stepped into the hallway with their rifles leveled and Scorpion in tow. Around the corner, Gizmo and Bicep squatted behind a howitzer, returning fire with their Tavors.

"Cease fire, idiots!" Scorpion shouted to his men. At last they saw him. The shooting stopped.

"Huddle up tight," Athena told her team.

They clustered around the arms dealer and moved for the exit. Outside, more of Scorpion's men waited with guns drawn. The guards yielded as I-6 shuffled for the truck with their captive. Gizmo started the engine as the others climbed aboard.

"Tell your men to drop their weapons and back away," Athena told Scorpion.

"If I refuse?"

She shrugged. "Then we'll have no choice but to take you with us."

Scorpion yelled, and his guards grudgingly complied.

Athena hopped onto the truck's bumper. "Move out."

They kept their Tavors ready as the truck pulled away, but no one from the camp made a move. Scorpion stood with his hands on his hips, watching them go.

CHAPTER 5

SETTING THE TRAP

The Showroom
Central Alps
0900 Local / 22 JUL

The corporate helicopter settled onto a landing pad. Zumi unbuckled from the soft leather seat. Cold air rushed into the cabin as an attendant opened the door. Zumi and Doc Dee stepped onto the helipad, ready for their visit to the Showroom.

Getting an appointment had been hard. Gizmo had used credentials from Viggo's laptop to make phony profiles on the dark web. The fake accounts had made

Zumi and Doc Dee appear to be military advisors to a notorious dictator. Director Ngata had helped by sending them garish uniforms from the dictator's army.

Now, Zumi tugged on the uniform's stiff collar. Her heavy brown jacket had red shoulder boards with golden trim. The large hat bore a colonel's insignia. At least it was warm. The high Alpine mountains stayed cold even in summer.

She surveyed the snow-covered peaks and whistled. "This place is gorgeous."

"Accessible only by chopper," Doc Dee noted. "I guess it cuts down on prying eyes."

A woman in a stylish, black trench coat approached. "Welcome," she said. "Please follow me."

Zumi and Doc Dee walked along a cobblestone path to the veranda of a

mansion. The elegant stone building looked as old as the mountains and just as magnificent.

Their guide punched a code into a keypad, unlocking a pair of polished wooden doors.

"Please browse at your leisure," she said. "If you have any questions, I am here."

Zumi and Doc Dee went through a foyer and down a long hall. Glass cases held a variety of pistols and hand grenades. A tiny card next to each item stated the price and quantity available.

The hall opened onto a grand ballroom with chandeliers and parquet flooring. Zumi imagined formal parties with couples dancing to the music of an orchestra. Today, the partygoers had been replaced by deadly tools of war.

Doc Dee pointed. "Missiles are over there."

They found the SA-18 Grouse display. The price card said the missile currently had just one seller.

"The seller has to be Viggo," Doc Dee whispered.

The woman in the trench coat sidled up to them. "May I offer assistance?"

"Yes," said Zumi. "We wish to make an SA-18 purchase."

"How many units?"

"The seller's entire inventory," Zumi replied.

The woman arched an eyebrow but said nothing. She took a satellite phone from her coat pocket and placed a call.

Zumi's nerves tensed. She had learned many skills as a soldier, but acting was not among them.

"This is Anna from the Showroom," the woman said into the phone. "I have buyers for your SA-18s, seeking all available units."

Zumi couldn't quite hear Viggo's response. But his tone sounded skeptical.

"They are officers of a government that has purchased from us before," Anna assured him. "Everything seems to be in order." She listened as Viggo outlined his terms of sale.

"He has fifty-nine missiles and twelve launchers," Anna said. "The cost is four million US dollars."

Zumi looked to the ceiling, pretending to mull over Viggo's price. "That's acceptable," she said at last.

Anna gave Viggo the good news, then ended the call. "I will ensure a quick and easy transaction," she said cheerfully.

"Simply leave payment with me, and your purchase will be delivered to the destination of your choice."

"No," Zumi said. "We wish to inspect the missiles in person with the seller. Then, if we are satisfied, we will pay him directly."

Anna's brow furrowed, but she recovered with a warm smile. "I guarantee your satisfaction."

"Nothing personal," replied Zumi. "But I have my orders. A face-to-face purchase only."

Anna placed another call and explained the unusual demand. When it seemed Viggo might refuse, Zumi extended a hand for the phone.

"May I?" Zumi took the phone and spoke into it. "Seller, this is your potential buyer. My army seeks a few trusted dealers to upgrade our weapons. Obviously, it would be a lucrative partnership. Are you interested?"

She waited for a reply. When it came, the gruff voice chilled her.

"Yes," rasped Viggo.

"Good. In that case, I ask you to deliver the missiles in person. You will be paid on the spot, and then we can discuss future purchases."

A long pause followed. Zumi had dangled the bait. Now she hoped Viggo would bite.

"We meet in twelve hours," he snarled. "Anna will give you the location. Don't be late."

"Excellent. My colleague and I look forward to—"

Viggo hung up.

CHAPTER 6

RISKY RENDEZVOUS

Industrial Port
Barcelona, Spain
2030 Local / 22 JUL

The meeting place turned out to be an abandoned warehouse on the Barcelona waterfront. Most of its windows were gone, and piles of junk littered the floor.

The team parked inside and set up their ambush. Gizmo joined the pigeons in the rafters for a commanding view of the warehouse floor. Holes in the rotting roof enabled him to monitor the street. Bicep hid behind a dilapidated forklift, while Athena crouched inside a steel barrel.

Zumi and Doc Dee grabbed their costumes from the back of their rental van. They pulled the clothes on.

"Contact," yelled Gizmo. "I've got an unmarked delivery truck approaching. I can see a driver and a passenger."

"Two people?" Doc Dee said. "I thought Viggo worked alone."

"He's suspicious, so he brought a friend," Zumi guessed.

They stood in the beams of the rental van's headlights, which shone through the entrance and danced on the water across the street. The delivery truck's front end appeared. It turned from the street and nosed into the building.

The driver stepped out and stood in the blazing headlights of his own vehicle. He was young, fit, and heavily armed. Zumi saw a compact assault rifle slung across his chest. He wore a tactical vest stuffed with grenades and spare clips.

"Who are you?" Zumi demanded.

The man said nothing. His eyes probed the shadowy corners of the warehouse.

"A mercenary," Doc Dee murmured.

Zumi subtly unbuttoned her hip holster.

The man whistled. Zumi heard the delivery truck's rear doors swing open. Four more mercenaries swept forward.

"What is the meaning of this?" Zumi shouted. "I demand an explanation!"

A man in a business suit slammed the passenger door. Zumi squinted against the headlights. He was tall and wiry, with dark hair combed straight back.

"My apologies," Viggo said. "I had to guard against ambush."

"This meeting was supposed to be a show of trust," Zumi said.

"In my work, trust is hard to come by."

Zumi's mind raced. Earlier, the team had crafted a backup plan in case of trouble. The plan, which relied on split-second timing, would have a better chance of success if the mercenaries were distracted.

"Have your men load the missiles into my van," she said.

Viggo's cold eyes scrutinized her. Zumi wondered if he saw through the ruse. She pushed her doubt aside and glowered.

"Where is my payment?" Viggo asked suspiciously.

"In the van," Zumi said. "We'll get it."

"No," Viggo snapped. He pulled a handgun and aimed at her. "Your aide can get it. You wait here with me."

Doc Dee and Zumi exchanged a glance. She nodded, almost imperceptibly, letting him know the plan was a go. Doc Dee's expression showed he understood.

"Get the money," Zumi said.

She began a silent countdown, giving Doc Dee ten seconds to get inside the van. The countdown reached zero.

"Now!" Zumi yelled, dropping to the ground.

Athena, Bicep, and Gizmo opened fire from their concealed positions. Muzzle flashes strobed in the shadows as bullets flew. The mercenaries reacted without hesitation, expertly returning fire as they hurried Viggo to cover. The exchange exploded into a fierce firefight.

Zumi, still flat on her belly, pulled her pistol from its holster and shot out the truck's headlights. Inside the van, Doc Dee flicked off its headlights, plunging the warehouse into darkness. I-6 now had a

tactical edge over the mercenaries. Zumi pictured Athena, Bicep, and Gizmo pulling down their night-vision goggles.

Viggo slid behind the delivery truck's steering wheel. He was trying to escape, leaving his men to fend for themselves. The truck began backing out of the warehouse.

"No!" Zumi aimed carefully for a tire.

The truck lurched but kept moving. She shot the other front tire. The truck backed onto the road and turned, then sluggishly started forward. Her final shot shattered the driver's side window. Zumi saw Viggo casually brush broken glass from his jacket as he pulled away.

The mercenaries appeared to be making a phased withdrawal, covering one another as they fell back for the exit. In three or four minutes, they'd be gone.

Zumi refused to wait. She crawled toward the van, grateful for her costume's thick wool jacket as she passed over glass shards and rusty nails.

Doc Dee helped her inside. "Are you okay?"

"I'm fine." Zumi closed the door behind her. "But we need to hurry before Viggo escapes."

Doc Dee peered out the van's window. "We'll be caught in that crossfire."

"He's getting away!" The urgency in Zumi's voice surprised even her.

"Okay," said Doc Dee. "Just go in the back and stay down."

He wedged himself between the driver and passenger seats, then turned the ignition and shifted into drive. With one hand on the wheel, Doc Dee peeked over the dash. The van crept forward.

"Here we go," he warned.

A torrent of bullets passed through the van's thin skin and continued out the other side. Zumi pressed her body against the cargo deck as shots ticked the metal frame. At last, the van exited the warehouse.

Zumi rolled onto her back. Streetlights shone through a constellation of bullet holes. Gizmo climbed into the driver's seat. The van accelerated.

"I shot out his front tires," Zumi called. "He couldn't have gotten very far."

"He didn't," Doc Dee replied, abruptly bringing the van to a halt.

Zumi flung open the door and stepped out. A crumpled guardrail lay at her feet.

In the dark water beyond, the delivery truck's roof slipped below the surface.

CHAPTER 7
TEAMWORK

Industrial Port
Barcelona, Spain
2245 Local / 22 JUL

The mercenaries had disengaged and vanished into the night. I-6 had chosen not to pursue. Their target was Viggo, not his hired soldiers.

Flashing lights had surrounded the warehouse as local police arrived. The teammates promptly dropped their weapons and raised their hands to avoid any misunderstanding. Athena spoke in Spanish with the chief inspector, who demanded an explanation for the bedlam.

The inspector's anger faded when he

learned of the team's target. A little chaos was tolerable if it meant capturing the notorious Viggo the Vulture.

Now, Zumi stood at the water's edge with Athena and the chief inspector. A huge crane lifted the sunken delivery truck from the harbor and set it before them. Ribbons of seaweed hung from the wheels and bumpers.

Zumi opened the driver's door. Water gushed out and a crab scuttled away, but there was no sign of Viggo.

"He did this on purpose, so we'd think he's dead," she said. Viggo's duplicity no longer surprised her.

The chief inspector frowned. "So this madman runs loose in my city?"

"I'm afraid so," said Athena. "Inspector, my team and I take full responsibility for Viggo's presence. He's here because of

us, and it's a problem we intend to fix. But we could use your help in containing him."

The inspector nodded. "I will set up checkpoints around the city. He will not escape."

Another rush of water splashed to the ground as officers opened the rear doors, revealing dozens of slender green crates.

"At least we got his missiles," Zumi said.

The chief inspector led I-6 to police headquarters and gave them a command bunker built for civil emergencies. The basement office had a kitchen, cots, and wall monitors with live feeds from security cams across the city.

Gizmo logged on to the team's secure network and placed a video call. Everyone cheered when a smiling Shade answered. He wore a navy-blue robe and sat in a hospital chair as early-evening light streamed through a nearby window.

"Look at this guy," Bicep quipped. "How do I get some of that soft duty?"

Shade laughed. "Be careful what you wish for. The physical therapy is kicking my butt."

The team updated Shade on the mission status. He listened intently as they described the warehouse firefight.

"So, basically, you've got a dangerous fugitive hiding in a city of more than five million people," Shade summarized.

"We thought our spy-craft expert might have advice for finding him," said Athena.

Shade rubbed his chin. "It's Viggo's move. He's laying low now, but soon he'll start looking for a way out of the city."

"How do you think he'll do it?" asked Gizmo.

"If it were me, I'd start by changing my appearance. Hair color, clothing style, facial hair, the works. A disguise would let me scout the police checkpoints."

"Viggo met us at the port, so we're wondering if he arrived by boat," Zumi said.

"Possibly," Shade said. "But he won't go back to the same boat since it could be compromised. He might try to get out on a fishing charter or a rental yacht."

"We'll keep the marina under tight surveillance," Athena said. "Where else should we look?"

"I like trains for covert travel because they're reliable, and the frequent stops give me an easy exit, if necessary."

"What about the airport?"

"That's a tough one," Shade said, again rubbing his chin. "Flying is the quickest way out, but airline passengers get more scrutiny than other travelers. Still, if he can slip through security, he's home free."

"We'll keep an eye on the airport," Athena said.

"Also," Shade said, "I want to speak with Director Ngata about using the CIA's facial-recognition software. It can see through the most-elaborate disguises."

Athena nodded. "I'll ask the local chief inspector about sharing his video feeds with Langley."

"One more thing," Shade said. "Viggo's paranoia will make him hard to corner. You need to be subtle. And when the time comes to spring the trap, be decisive."

"We will," Zumi said. "Stay on top of your physical therapy. We need you ready for the next mission."

"Count on it," Shade said with a smile.

CHAPTER 8

SURVEILLANCE OPERATION

Josep Tarradellas
Barcelona–El Prat Airport
Barcelona, Spain
1330 Local / 26 JUL

The I-6 team donned street clothes and deployed across the city. Doc Dee watched the marina, while Athena, Bicep, and Gizmo prowled the three busiest rail stations. Zumi took the airport, spending her days in the security office staring at a bank of monitors.

She yawned. Today was her fourth day of watching passengers put their bags on conveyor belts and step through body scanners. Occasionally a possible match for Viggo appeared, but closer inspection always ruled the person out.

"Go grab some lunch, guys," Zumi said in Spanish.

The chief inspector had assigned her two officers from the Grup Especial d'Intervenció, or GEI, the local equivalent of SWAT. These men were skilled in anti-terrorism tactics. On the first day, they had been alert and ready for action. But as the long hours passed, they grew bored and restless, just like Zumi.

"Can we get you anything?" one asked.

"No, I'll—"

A radio call interrupted. Gizmo was reporting a probable match at his train station.

"Hold on, guys," Zumi said, turning up the volume. "We may have something."

"How sure are you, Gizmo?" radioed Athena.

"Well, the hair is different, and he's dressed like a tourist," Gizmo said. "But the facial features look right. I really think it's Viggo."

"What's he doing?" Athena asked.

"He just walked past a security cam. I'm uploading a screenshot."

Zumi grabbed her tablet. An image appeared of a busy train station. In the foreground, a tall, lanky man peered over his shoulder. He had curly blond hair and a polo shirt. His casual look contrasted sharply with the slick businessman Zumi had met in the warehouse. Still, he seemed familiar. She enlarged the image and saw those same cold eyes.

"It's him," Zumi said. The GEI officers leaned over her shoulder for a closer look.

She pressed the radio's talk button. "It's him. I know it!"

"Okay," said Athena. "I'm sending this image to Langley for confirmation. In the meantime, we'll assume we've got eyes on Viggo."

"He just stepped onto a boarding platform," Gizmo reported.

"Gizmo, you need to get on that train," Athena said. "Remember to keep your distance. We'll set up a rotating surveillance op."

The I-6 team began to converge on their target. Gizmo boarded the train car behind Viggo's, where he could take quick peeks through a narrow window. Doc Dee, meanwhile, left the marina and rushed to the nearest train station. Athena and Bicep prepared to move as well.

Their plan was to rotate observers so

Viggo would never realize he was being followed. The complicated surveillance operation needed a quarterback, someone who could watch the big picture and direct the others. Zumi found herself in a perfect position for that role.

The airport security office had access to a digital railway map showing the real-time movement of trains around the city. Zumi pulled up the map on a big wall monitor, then identified the train carrying Viggo and Gizmo. Next, she wrote each teammate's name on a piece of tape and labeled their locations. She took a deep breath. Now it was time to start calling plays.

"The target is two stops away from Doc Dee's station," she said into the radio. "Gizmo will hand off surveillance to Doc Dee."

"Roger," they both said.

Zumi instructed Doc Dee to buy a newspaper and pretend to read it. Viggo had gotten a good look at him in the warehouse, so Doc Dee needed to hide his face. The handoff took place as planned. Doc Dee boarded the train and took over surveillance as Gizmo exited.

Athena broke in on the radio. "We now have CIA confirmation that this is Viggo. Repeat: the man with curly blond hair and a polo shirt is Viggo in disguise."

"He's standing up," Doc Dee said. "I think he's getting ready to leave the train."

"Bicep, the target is getting off at your stop," said Zumi. "You'll need to shadow him on foot."

"Understood. I see the train arriving now."

Bicep trailed Viggo through the busy

station to another boarding platform, then followed him onto a new train.

“Where does this guy think he’s going?” Gizmo wondered.

Zumi traced Viggo’s path with her finger. “He’s taking a convoluted route, hoping to shake any tails.”

“Do you think he's spotted us?”

She studied the map. “Negative. I think he’s just being cautious.”

Viggo switched trains twice more. Zumi managed to keep a tail on him, but the transfers forced her to reuse observers, which was risky. Presently, Athena trailed Viggo on foot through yet another station.

“Stand by,” Athena radioed. “He just boarded the airport train.”

Zumi’s eyes darted to the map. “There are no more stops on that line. He’s coming here. Repeat: his destination is the airport."

Behind her, the GEI officers started gearing up. As they strapped on body armor and checked their PSG1 sniper rifles, Zumi turned to them.

"I've seen Viggo in action," she said. "He is ruthless and remarkably cunning, a man who will do anything to escape. Our goal is to take him alive, but don't hesitate to shoot if innocent lives are at risk."

The officers nodded and hurried out the door.

Zumi got back on the radio. "Athena has eyes on the target. Everyone else needs to hustle to the airport. The snipers have been deployed."

She glanced to the flashing red line that represented the airport train. "Hurry. Viggo will be here in twelve minutes."

CHAPTER 9

SHOWDOWN

Josep Tarradellas
Barcelona–El Prat Airport
Barcelona, Spain
1515 Local / 26 JUL

The train arrived. Passengers departed. Throngs of travelers made their way to the check-in counters. Zumi scanned the monitors and found Viggo. She also spotted Athena lurking in the background.

As Viggo stood in line, the other I-6 members arrived at the airport and trickled into the office. Once Viggo passed through security screening, Athena joined them. Now Zumi could begin her briefing. She went to the large wall monitor and called up a diagram of the airport.

"Viggo is making his way through Terminal 2," she said. "The scanners didn't find any weapons, so he's unarmed. And he must be feeling relaxed, because he just stopped for coffee and a sandwich."

The bank of monitors showed Viggo seated at a table, casually enjoying lunch.

"Do we know where he's headed?" Doc Dee asked.

"He checked in to Caliber flight 3834, which boards from Gate R14 in twenty minutes."

"What about the snipers?" Bicep asked.

"They're hidden from view, moving into position via a service corridor."

Gizmo pointed. "Looks like our boy just finished his chow."

The camera showed Viggo glancing

over his shoulder before disappearing into a restroom.

“Okay, people, this is it,” Athena said. “We’ll take him at the gate. Stay out of sight until I give the word. We should be able to do this without firing a shot.”

Everyone prepared to move out. They were leaving the office when Zumi gasped. “Where did he get that bag?”

The monitor showed Viggo walking away from the restroom with a small pack on his shoulder.

“He didn’t have it when he went in,” Gizmo said.

“No, he certainly did not,” said Doc Dee. “Someone must have left it there for him.”

Bicep frowned. “Probably bribed or threatened an airport worker. Now what?”

“Now the job gets much more difficult,” Athena said. “Everyone is cleared to shoot, but be mindful of civilians. The terminal is packed."

They left the security office and dashed down the service corridor. Zumi radioed the snipers as she ran, warning them that Viggo was likely armed. The GEI officers replied that they had climbed into an air duct above the boarding area. They could see Viggo below, waiting for his flight with the other passengers.

I-6 reached the doorway leading to the concourse. As they caught their breath, Zumi cracked the door and peeked out.

"Viggo is in a long row of seats about twenty meters away," she told the others. "He's hunched over the backpack. His hands are inside it."

"Our best chance for a clean capture is to rush him," Athena said. "Get ready to swarm."

The team lined at the door. Zumi radioed the snipers it was time. She inhaled deeply and felt her pulse quicken.

"Execute," Athena said.

As they stormed the concourse, time shifted into slow motion. Zumi could see every detail, including the startled faces of nearby travelers. Other travelers were blissfully unaware, chatting and laughing, oblivious to the drama about to unfold.

Viggo spotted the team instantly. His hands emerged from the backpack with a compact submachine gun.

"Get down!" Zumi yelled in Spanish.

A few travelers dived to the floor, but most simply stared in confusion. Viggo leaped from his seat and vaulted behind a customer service desk. People saw the black submachine gun in his hands. Their screams triggered a stampede.

Porte
Gate
Puerta
R 14

The surge of people drove Zumi backward. She pushed through it, like a salmon swimming upstream, then jumped onto a luggage cart. At that instant, Viggo began spraying bullets. One passed so close to Zumi's cheek she could feel its tiny shock wave.

Flashes from the ceiling told her the GEI officers had opened fire. Zumi looked up and saw their muzzles protruding from the air vents. One of the snipers scored a hit, knocking Viggo to the floor with an apparent shoulder injury. The shooting abated, leaving an eerie silence.

Afternoon sunshine lit the wall of windows behind the service desk. Zumi squinted as she and the others crept closer, using the long rows of seats for cover. With hand signals, Athena arranged her team in a semicircle, then motioned them forward. They would surround the desk, pinning Viggo against the wall and leaving him no escape.

Zumi heard the click of a magazine being loaded. "Cover!" she hissed, rolling beneath the nearest seats.

Viggo opened up yet again, but this time he ignored the team. He fired at the overhead vents that hid the snipers. Thick chunks of drywall and ceiling tile rained down as bullets shredded the ventilation system. The ductwork gave way and crashed to the floor.

"No!" Zumi shouted.

She ran toward the debris. Doc Dee did the same. Together, they pulled apart smashed, bullet-riddled ductwork as the rest of the team provided covering fire. Viggo bolted from behind the desk. He was on the move again.

Zumi feared what she might find. But when she pulled back the final piece of sheet metal, she sighed in relief. Both GEI officers were banged up but alive.

"Looks like some broken bones and flesh wounds," Doc Dee said after a quick assessment. "Their body armor really did its job."

"How can I help?" Zumi asked.

"I'll handle it. Go help the others subdue Viggo."

Zumi looked around. The boarding area was quiet and empty. The terrorist had managed to slip away yet again.

"Here," said one of the GEI officers as he pulled off his vest. "Take this for protection."

Zumi forced a smile and took the armored vest. "You did great, guys. I'll make sure we get him."

CHAPTER 10

HIJACK ATTACK

Terminal 2, Gate R14
Barcelona Airport
1600 Local / 26 JUL

Viggo's shoulder wound had left blood droplets behind the customer service desk. Zumi followed the crimson trail down a boarding gangway and onto an A320 jetliner. Athena, Gizmo, and Bicep stood before the jet's locked cockpit.

"Viggo ran in there." Gizmo nodded at the cockpit door.

"Let's just wait him out," Zumi suggested. "The plane is empty, and he can't stay in there forever."

Athena shook her head. "We heard shouting. The pilots must have been doing their preflight checks. So, he's got hostages."

The whine of turbine engines began.

"Hostages who can be forced to fly him out of here," said Bicep. "Viggo is about to add hijacking to his list of terrorist achievements."

Gizmo grimaced. "A hijacked plane is an airborne weapon. The Spanish Air Force will be forced to shoot it down."

The engines grew louder.

Athena closed the exit door, locking them inside the plane. "No," she said firmly. "We can't let that happen. Give me ideas for getting into that cockpit."

Zumi shook her head. "Cockpit doors are like bank vaults. They can stand up to gunfire and hand grenades."

“Even if we could blast our way in, it would be too risky for the pilots,” Bicep said.

The plane began moving. It taxied for the nearest runway.

Gizmo studied a keypad next to the door. “How much does Viggo know about aircraft?”

“He’s no doubt an expert on military aircraft,” said Zumi. “But civilian jetliners? Probably not much.”

“What did you have in mind, Gizmo?” asked Athena.

“Well, I can use this keypad to signal the pilots to unlock the door. Viggo might not realize they can do it remotely, without leaving their seats.”

The plane reached the runway. Its engines roared to full throttle for takeoff.

“Okay,” said Athena. “Once the cockpit

door is unlocked, we'll need a nonlethal option for subduing Viggo. A shootout could be disastrous."

"How about a flashbang?" said Bicep.

Zumi wrinkled her brow. "Where would we get a stun grenade?"

"From you," he said, pointing.

She looked down at the borrowed vest and smiled sheepishly. An M84 stun grenade was clipped to it.

"It's a good idea," Athena said. "But that tiny cockpit will magnify the stun effects. I'm worried about the pilots."

The jet sped down the runway and climbed into the air.

"I guarantee that fighter jets are being scrambled as we speak," Gizmo warned.

Athena nodded. "Let's do it."

Zumi unclipped the flashbang. With a tight grip on the arming lever, she pulled its two pins, then looked to Gizmo. He tapped a door-unlock request into the keypad. They waited.

A red light on the keypad turned green. They heard a soft metallic whir. Athena placed her hand on the door handle and turned. It was unlocked.

Zumi inched closer. Time slowed again as Athena opened the door. Zumi glanced inside the cockpit and saw the pilots in their seats. Viggo stood behind them with his back to the doorway. He was just starting to turn when she tossed in the grenade. Athena slammed the door shut.

The next three seconds seemed to last forever. Zumi wondered if the grenade was a dud, but then she heard its thunderous boom. It was much louder for the cockpit's occupants. They would also be experiencing a blinding flash.

Athena opened the door once more. Viggo lay on the floor. The pilots were slumped in their seats. Bicep rushed in and grabbed the terrorist by the collar, then dragged him from the cockpit and bound his arms and legs.

Zumi checked the pilots. "They're out cold."

The aircraft was still in its takeoff climb.

"How long until they recover?" asked Athena.

"It was a heavier stun than usual," Zumi said. "I don't know how long the effects will linger."

Athena eyed the bright blue sky. "Can you level us off?"

Zumi bit her lip. "I've had a few lessons in a Cessna, but I'm no pilot. Not even close."

“I get it,” Athena said. “But we need you to try.”

Zumi scanned the cockpit. A few dials and controls seemed familiar, but most were a mystery. “I’ll do my best,” she said at last.

Bicep and Gizmo carried the pilots to the passenger cabin. Zumi sat down. The altimeter showed six thousand meters and climbing. She nudged the control stick forward until the plane leveled off.

At that instant, a fighter jet roared past. Zumi recognized it as a Eurofighter Typhoon. The jet had Spanish Air Force markings and carried air-to-air missiles. The nimble fighter streaked ahead and turned sharply, as if preparing to launch a missile.

Zumi pulled on a headset, which was already dialed to the emergency channel.

"Attention, Caliber flight 3834," the Typhoon pilot called. "Return to the airport immediately. If you fail to comply, I am authorized to fire."

Zumi pressed the talk button. "Typhoon, this is Caliber 3834. You are speaking with an American special operator, call sign Zumi. You can confirm my identity with airport security."

"Stand by, Caliber."

A moment passed as the fighter pilot conferred with authorities on the ground. When he came back on the emergency channel, his tone had softened. "Roger, Zumi. Identity confirmed. Please advise on your status."

"Viggo is in custody, but the plane's pilots have been temporarily incapacitated. We need help getting back on the ground."

"Understood, Zumi. I will assist." The Typhoon glided in front of the airliner's nose. "You can follow me all the way down."

Zumi had questions for him about using the throttle and floor pedals. As they descended toward the airport, he advised her on lowering the flaps and landing gear.

The runway came into view.

"Stay with me, Zumi," the fighter pilot encouraged. "We are almost there."

"Roger," she said. "I'm ready."

The runway stretched before her. Zumi eased the throttle and stick, waiting for her wheels to touch down. The tires hit the concrete a bit harder than she would have liked. The big jet bounced twice before settling into a steady roll.

As the aircraft came to a stop, a fleet

of fire trucks and ambulances surrounded it with lights flashing. Zumi shut down the engines and leaned back with a sigh.

"Outstanding job," said Athena, handing her a cold bottle of water from the galley. "We just might lose you to the airlines."

CIA Headquarters
Langley, Virginia
0930 Local / 30 SEP

Zumi waited in the cavernous lobby. A wall-mounted TV showed live coverage of Viggo's trial at The Hague, Netherlands. The terrorist sat handcuffed to a table, glowering at a prosecutor who recited a long list of crimes.

"Looks like the Vulture will never fly again," said a familiar voice.

Zumi turned to greet Shade, who seemed his old self, except for his clothes. She had never seen him in a business suit.

"How's life behind a desk?" she asked.

Shade shrugged. "Not bad. We're still analyzing the data from Viggo's hideout. I predict many more terrorists will soon be sitting in courtrooms."

"When will you be able to rejoin I-6?"

"I made a deal with my doctors," Shade said. "Three more weeks of wearing suits, and they'll certify me as mission-ready."

"Awesome," Zumi said with a smile. "Now, tell me why I'm here today."

"Last time, we had to leave in a hurry. I thought you might enjoy a proper tour."

Shade led her across the lobby to a

white marble wall with dozens of stars. "Each star represents a CIA employee who died in the line of service. Many of these spies remain anonymous, even in death."

He showed her a display of spy artifacts, some dating back to the Revolutionary War. Then they walked through the gardens. Zumi saw statues and other solemn tributes to American secret agents.

"The CIA has a long memory." Shade paused before a rustic waterfall. "This is where they honor friends and allies."

Zumi stepped closer to the waterfall. Symbols were etched into its boulders. The nearest stone had a fresh carving.

Smiling, she reached out and traced the familiar insignia—the number six with parts marked out of it.

GEAR SPOTLIGHT

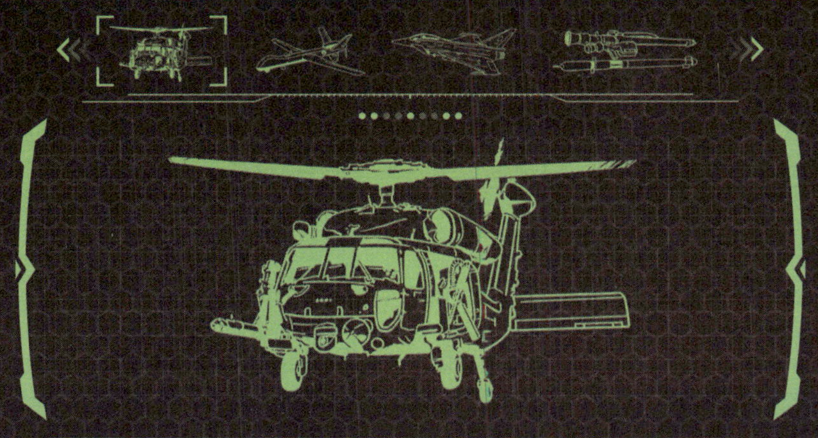

HH-60 Pave Hawk

This helicopter's main tasks are to enter unsafe areas and recover military personnel, perform search-and-rescue operations, and provide aid during disasters.

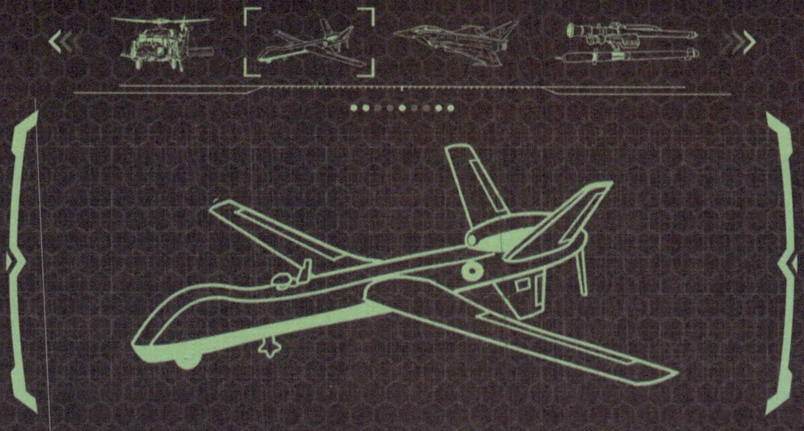

MQ-9 Reaper

This remote-controlled aircraft can attack time-sensitive targets. It can carry air-to-ground Hellfire missiles that make accurate strikes without causing much collateral damage.